ACCEPTING THE MOON

K. S. HAIGWOOD

Accepting the Moon

ISBN-13: 978-1502370730
ISBN-10: 1502370735

Edited by: Ella Medler
Interior Design & Layout: Deena Rae @ E-BookBuilders
        Interior images modified or created by E-Bookbuilders
        Tribal Moon image from Clipartbest.com/clipart-dc6ARqdc9

DEDICATION

For the voices. If it wasn't for you, I wouldn't be me.

TABLE OF CONTENTS

CHAPTER 1

MENA

Twelve years.

The silence was deafening as I stared at him through shimmering tears, waiting—waiting for *that* answer, an answer I already knew to be true. I was torturing myself by doing it but, for some reason, I had to know. Why didn't I just turn and walk away? Would hearing him say it actually make me feel any better? It wouldn't change the past, it wouldn't change what he did and it damn sure wouldn't change my mind about leaving him, so why the hell was I still standing before him, trembling with anger and humility and waiting for him to respond to my question?

Twelve years wasted. It was all I could think about; that, and the fact that I was scared to death, because I had no idea what I was going to do. In a single, heart-stopping moment of weakness, he had chosen to erase everything we had ever had together, everything we had worked for and everything we had become. Everything was just… gone.

Because of her. Because of him. Because of what they did together!

I wanted to scream and shout at him to say something, but the words were stuck somewhere on the other side of the huge lump in my throat.

The guilt and shame were clear on his face, but it didn't matter to me that he regretted anything—or that he merely pretended to. I would never be able to look at him the same, even if I could somehow muster up enough compassion to forgive him for stealing the best years of my life and throwing them back in my face as if I was nothing important to him at all.

My breath hitched in my throat and I jerked back when he took a step toward me. His frame went rigid and his left hand remained extended out to me as if silently pleading with me to stay.

Nervous brown eyes followed my gaze to where I had placed a platinum wedding band twelve years earlier, and he swore under his breath at the sight of the slightly lighter shade of skin there, at the base of his ring finger.

The blood drained from his face as the brimming tears cascaded down my cheeks.

"Mena, I never meant—"

"Was it worth it?" I whispered, cutting his lie short.

He exhaled slowly as he turned away from me, that left hand coming up again, but this time so he could run his fingers through his hair—hair that I had only just noticed had begun to recede and turn gray a bit at the temples.

He sighed as he pinched the bridge of his nose and exhaled loudly. "I don't know what to say."

"How about the truth? After what you've done, don't I deserve at least that much?"

He sighed again, and I dug half moons in the palms of my hands in the long, uncomfortable silence that followed.

"I'm sorry."

I waited for him to continue, to say something—anything—else. Nothing came. He just stood there, avoiding eye contact and waiting for me to—to what? Say, 'Okay, you are forgiven?' Bullshit!

"What?" I said, and my voice cracked in disbelief or anger; I wasn't absolutely sure which. It could have been both. "Exactly what are you sorry about, Marc? Lying to me? Destroying our marriage? Sleeping with another woman?" I screamed the last question at him and involuntarily bent at the waist. Dizziness and a wave of nausea took over my body at the thought of him, my husband of twelve years, having sex with another woman.

Where had I gone wrong?

He touched my shoulder and I quickly moved out of his reach.

Glaring up at him through my dark lashes, I took another guarded step back and forced myself to stand upright. "Don't you dare touch me."

"Christ, Mena, I never meant for anything to happen! It just—shit! It just did. She meant—she means—nothing to me," he finished softly, and his eyes begged me to believe the lie.

Trembling from head to toe, I rubbed my hands up and down my arms, desperately trying to chase away the queasy feeling in the pit of my stomach.

"How did we get to this place? I feel like I don't even know you anymore," I whispered.

He huffed, but seemed relieved that I had decided to stay and talk things through. I suppose he still thought he had a fighting chance. "I know.

I don't know you, either, Mena, but I want to. We've grown apart. We've changed—everyone changes," he stressed.

A collage of wedding photos hung above the fireplace mantle behind him, and I stared at the frames without really seeing the memories frozen behind their glasses. A girl's wedding day is supposed to be the happiest day of her life, but I barely even remembered mine.

"This wasn't in the plan," I said. "This was not supposed to happen to me." I knew that seemed so cliché of me to say, and I knew people cheated on their spouses all the time, but I honestly never thought it would happen to me.

"I know," he said again. "I'm so sorry, baby. Please—"

My eyes widened in surprise. "Please? Please what, Marc? Forgive you?" I laughed sarcastically. "How? Tell me how I am supposed to ever be able to trust that you won't do this again." I shook my head. "No—I don't think I will forgive you for this—not today… not ever."

I think he realized in that moment that I had no intentions of staying with him. Did he think I was ignorant?

Swallowing hard, he took a hesitant step toward me. "We can get through this, baby. I promise I will never hurt you again. I'll make this better if you'll just let me. I love you," he whispered, and even managed to keep eye contact with me.

How many lies had he told that I never saw through to the real man he was: a deceiving, mind-manipulating, cheating bastard.

Yes. He thought I was ignorant. And I guess I had been, but I wasn't going to be any longer. I refused to lie to myself every day while knowing, deep down inside, that he would do it again and again.

I let him take another step closer while I turned the two-carat diamond engagement ring to the inside of my hand with my thumb.

"How could you do this to me, to us?"

He shook his head and moved into my personal space. "I didn't realize how much you mean to me. I know now. It will never happen again," he said, his voice shaking with emotion. If I hadn't caught him in so many lies already, I might have believed he was genuinely upset. "I need you, Mena."

"You should have thought of that before you put your wedding band in your pocket and screwed someone other than your wife!"

In an instant, his expression turned sour and I couldn't get my arm up in time to block the blow from the back of his hand across my cheekbone. I was too stunned to cry out. He had never hit me before.

3

I whimpered as my hand hovered shakily over the throbbing area under my eye. I knew I needed to pull myself together. I couldn't let him beat me without a fight. I refused to let him have that sort of control over me.

"I hate myself for hurting you like that, Mena, but I said I was sorry, damn it! You should have just accepted the apology and forgiven me. Do you think this is fun for me? Do you think I enjoy hurting you?"

With so much adrenaline rushing through me, it had been difficult to stay calm while he made it sound like him hitting me was my fault. I couldn't hold it back any longer, and I nearly missed the look of shock in his eyes before my left hand slapped him hard across his right cheek.

Bright red blood poured freely from the long gash my ring had carved in his cheek, and he looked at me in horror as I grinned menacingly at him.

"Explain that to your whore. Your wife is leaving you."

CHAPTER 2

JAXON

Jaxon scanned the growing crowd of the club with guarded eyes.

Puppets, every last damn one of them, he thought.

Shaking his head, he slapped a twenty and the empty old fashioned glass on the bar hard enough to get the bartender's attention over the raging, death-metal music that was the club's entertainment for the night.

"Another double?" the bartender asked, and Jaxon nudged the glass with the tips of his fingers to encourage the pouring of the sweet, burning poison.

He smelled the approaching human before he heard her voice, and his lips curved up at the corners as she took the seat beside him. It appeared she was going to make it easy for him.

"I haven't seen you in here before. You from out of town?" the female voice shouted over the noise pollution.

Not really, but he couldn't hunt in the same area too often or eyebrows would start to rise. He wasn't about to tell her any of that, though.

"I'm visiting a friend," Jaxon shouted back as he turned his head, flashing his million dollar smile at the girl. She looked to be in her early twenties, pretty, bleached-blond hair, maybe a little too thin and a bit over the top in the make-up department, but she would do. He didn't want her body, after all.

He offered her his hand to shake, but when she took it, he brought her knuckles up to his lips for a tender kiss, keeping eye contact with her the whole time.

She swooned, and he grinned as he released her fingers.

"Is your friend here at the club?" She glanced to his other side, obviously making sure there wasn't another woman sitting there that had already staked her claim on him. She smiled when she found the spot empty.

To her obvious delight, Jaxon shook his head. "I'm Brandon," he lied. "And you are?"

5

She sighed heavily as her eyelashes fluttered and her glossy eyes focused on his. "Yours for the night, if you'll get me away from all this noise and smoke. I wasn't quite expecting," she winced and cupped her hands over her ears as she shouted, "this. My friends insisted we come see *The Fighting Tarsier*."

He grinned and ran his fingers lightly over her knee. She inched closer, encouraging the forward gesture. "Your place?" Jaxon said.

She grimaced in what appeared to be actual pain. "I live with my parents."

Jaxon's lips flattened into a tight line as he wondered if she was really even old enough to be in a club. His head jerked once in the direction of the exit sign. "I've got a room at a motel a few blocks from here. C'mon." He stood, grabbed his jacket from the back of the stool and led her through the crowd of jumping bodies. He was sure he had never seen dancing quite like that before, not in the last two centuries anyway, and never in the United States.

She appeared to be delighted with the idea of leaving the club with a total stranger, but Jaxon honestly couldn't care less about where she placed her standards. He only needed one tiny, meaningless thing from her, and then he would send her on her merry little way.

"Do we need a cab?" The blonde asked as they stepped out into the frigid January air.

Jaxon shook his head. "If you don't mind the cold and a little bit of misty rain for a mile or two, we can take my bike. The motel is about ten or twelve blocks that way." He nodded to the west, toward the bad side of town, and Blondie, all of a sudden, didn't look all that enthused about leaving with him anymore. She glanced longingly toward the street and a passing cab.

He closed the distance between them and lifted her chin with one of his fingers, turning on his charm. "It's safe. I promise no harm will come to you. You can trust me."

She nodded once, then took his hand and let him lead her around the corner of the club to the alleyway.

Jaxon could have taken what he needed from the girl then and there, but the risk of being seen was too high and, as second in command under Phoenix, he couldn't afford to screw things up… again.

The slight drizzle had become a downpour by the time Jaxon parked his bike at the motel he used for special occasions, such as this one.

It wasn't the Ritz-Carlton, or even a Motel 8, but there weren't any cracks under the door and the roaches were pretty small. He never stayed more than half an hour, so spending the thirty-eight dollars for four walls out of sight suited him just fine. He wasn't the only male who paid for rooms by the hour, although his reasons were quite different from the other lowlifes he'd seen coming and going.

They ran underneath the short awning over the office door and Jaxon pushed his way inside. The girl tugged her hand free of his and held her cell phone up when he turned to see why she had stopped.

"Go on ahead. I'll wait for you right here. I just need to text my friends and let them know I left the club. I wouldn't want them to worry about me."

He eyed her a moment longer, thinking the second he turned his back she would bolt, but the night was still early and he could just wait for one of the hookers to drunkenly stumble out of one of the other rooms if his prey scurried away, so he gave her a nod and turned toward the man behind the counter to get his room key.

CHAPTER 3

MENA

I scrambled to find the wiper switch again and quickly realized the blades were already wiping the sheets of rain from the windshield as fast as they could. As if not being able to see through the storm wasn't problem enough, I couldn't seem to keep my tear ducts from leaking and blurring my vision even further.

"Stupid, cheating bastard," I mumbled under my breath, and wiped the dampness from my burning cheeks with a tissue.

I refused to say, 'What else can possibly go wrong?'. Out loud anyway. I already had the feeling Karma was kicked back with popcorn and laughing out loud at the obstacles she was throwing at me. Giving the bitch a challenge was not on my list of things to do.

Up ahead, a massive animal darted across the road and was out of sight before I could tell what the thing was. A wolf, maybe? It wasn't uncommon to see one up north, on the outskirts of the mountains, but in the city? I had never even heard of a sighting. Maybe it was only a large dog, I thought.

I eased off the accelerator just in case it had friends about to follow. Hitting an animal of that size could do some serious damage to a car, and I didn't need to be stranded in the bad part of the city in a storm with a wrecked vehicle and an injured, pissed off wolf just waiting for me to open the driver's door of my Audi.

I laughed a little at the image my imagination had dreamed up, and then screamed as I slammed on my brakes and cut the wheel, desperately trying to keep my car on the slick pavement and avoid hitting anything in the process.

The Audi finally came to a stop and was pointed in the direction I had come from. I hadn't hit anything. There wasn't much to hit; there wasn't a lot of traffic through this area, especially at one-thirty in the morning.

"Jesus," I whispered as I covered my pounding heart with my hand.

There had been so many of them—at least a dozen or more.

The police! The police would know what to do, I thought, and then reached for my cell phone. It wasn't in the console, where I always kept it while driving. I quickly turned on the interior lighting and checked the floorboards to see if the device had fallen during my driving escapade.

My eyes closed and I groaned when I realized I had placed it on the nightstand beside the bed before packing some of my things, and in my haste to get out and away from Marc…

I covered my face with my hands and cried. My cell was still at home.

The sound of a horn blaring brought me out of my stupor, and my heart shot up in my throat as I looked up to see the headlights of a semi heading right for me. The Audi was still in drive, so I shoved the accelerator to the floorboard and raced to get out of the road before I was flattened by the big truck.

The nauseating feeling was back full-force as I rolled to a stop in a motel parking lot.

Struggling through the overwhelming dizziness that fogged my brain, I eventually came to the conclusion that it was not safe for me to be behind the wheel, at least not until I calmed down—and the storm blew over. I realized I had only two options as I stared up at the flashing *vacancy* sign: use the office phone to call my brother to come get me or rent a room in the place and attempt to start over in the morning.

If I knew Marc at all, he wouldn't let this go; as a respected lawyer of the community, his reputation was too important to him to let the fact that he was an adulterer go public. He would look for me, and he wouldn't find me here.

I looked at the rundown dump of a motel and winced. Sometimes the worst things in life were a blessing in disguise.

I drew in a deep breath and turned my Audi in the direction of the motel's office.

I had to rent a room.

CHAPTER 4

JAXON

Jaxon paid cash for the room and took the key from the uninterested-looking attendant, then turned on his heel and walked toward the only exit in the room.

Seeing a bright red umbrella through the glass door stopped him before he even reached it. He watched in amusement as the human female fought with the object against the battering winds of the ever-growing storm. He had half a mind to leave the girl he had brought with him and seduce this one.

She was feisty, and pretty—just his type, actually—but if she couldn't win against a piece of light metal and a few strips of nylon, then she wouldn't have a chance against him. He liked them with a little fight in them.

He pondered his thought, and then chuckled lightly when the winds flipped the umbrella inside out and the female struggled to hang on to the damn thing.

A big gust of wind blew the door inward, and in with the breeze came a mouth-watering fragrance he wanted to taste on his tongue as soon as inhumanly possible.

Yes, Jaxon thought, this female would be leaving with him tonight, and they wouldn't be staying in this dump.

Without turning back to the guy behind the counter, Jaxon dropped the brass key in the dropbox and walked toward the woman.

"Here, let me help you, ma'am," he said, using his most charming accent as he took the umbrella from her and closed it up tight. "The storm is getting worse, but I actually think the umbrella is conspiring against you—" His eyes grew wide as she turned her full gaze on him. Her eyes were a stunning shade of pale green, but they weren't what had his attention.

She grabbed the umbrella out of his hand and threw it in the trash beside him. "It isn't the only thing that is conspiring against me tonight.

11

Thank you for taming the stubborn brolly for me, but it was actually the least of my problems. I think I could have managed to handle that one."

The girl went to move past him, but Jaxon stepped in the way, stopping her from walking out of his life, at least for the moment.

"Are you all right? Have you been in an accident?" His hand came up and his fingers caressed the delicate skin under her chin as he tugged her face up to get a better look at the swollen and heavily bruised area over her cheekbone. "Your eye—"

She huffed and backed away, intentionally turning her head so he couldn't see the injury. "Yes, I've been in an accident for twelve years. Now, if you would be so kind as to move out of my way, I need to rent a room in this fine establishment for the night, so I can at least get myself dry."

Confused, Jaxon raised an eyebrow and glanced around the outside of the motel, wondering if she was half blind or full-blown senile—neither would stop him from getting what he wanted from her—then he glanced back to what she was wearing: nothing on her person would have cost less than two-hundred dollars. Yes, he concluded, those were most definitely diamonds in her ears—real ones. Something wasn't adding up.

He leaned in close to her and whispered, "Are you on medication?"

The girl's eyes popped wide in what appeared to be shock or disbelief at the words he had spoken to her. "Are you insane—"

Jaxon shook his head. "Not that I'm aware of but, with all due respect, lady, I wasn't the one—" sniff-sniff "We need to go," he said in a rushed voice as he grabbed the car keys from her hand and pointed the keyless entry device toward the row of vehicles. The lights flashing on the Audi didn't surprise him; it was the nicest vehicle on the lot. He grabbed her hand and pulled her out into the storm.

CHAPTER 5

MENA

"What?" I shouted, and tried to pull my hand free of the maniac, but I may as well have been trying to pull a stubborn jackass out of quicksand with how well I was achieving the task. "Let me go!" I demanded, and swatted him with my purse.

He didn't even flinch.

"I'm not going with you," I said, and even sounded convincing to my own ears, but obviously not to his, because he opened the passenger door of my Audi then turned and effortlessly picked me up in his arms, like one would a child.

I screamed for help but the plea sounded small up against all the rain and thundering. I was going to die, I thought. He was going to kidnap me and rape me and cut me up into little pieces and kill me. Dead!

I was too scared to cry; either that or I was in shock. And even through all the kicking and slapping I was doing to my abductor to try and get away, what I had done to piss Karma off so badly was in the forefront of my mind. I mean, C'mon! What the hell had I done? Nobody deserved this much bad luck!

Suddenly I realized my attacker had gone still and I was the only one fighting. Well, I had been the only one fighting all along, but now it seemed the barbarian had stopped resisting.

Was he going to let me go?

A low growl cut through the sharp winds and my head jerked around at the sound.

The animals I had seen crossing the road in front of my vehicle had surrounded the car... and us.

"Oh, shit! Put me in the car! Hurry! Put me in the car, now!"

"Be quiet," the guy growled out through a tight jaw.

"Don't tell me to be quiet!" My arm flew out and I pointed in a random direction. It would pretty much do the trick; we were completely confined.

"Those wolves are about to eat us!" I exclaimed as if he was slow and couldn't comprehend that simple, yet obvious fact.

None of the beasts moved. They only glared at us with their teeth bared, waiting for their prey to run.

"Please, just be still. I swear I will do everything in my power to get us out of this situation alive."

I laughed then. "You! You're going to get us out of this alive? Ha! Not hardly. What power do you have besides the strength of a caveman? I'm surprised you didn't drag me to the car by my hair!"

A wolf snarled and inched closer. The others followed suit.

"Oh, God," I said, and then was slung around to his back.

"Sorry. I'm gonna need my hands for this. Hang on to me."

Was he seriously going to fight them?

He crouched, and I squeaked as I hid my face in his neck.

Please don't let this be real. I'm not ready to die. It has to be a dream. That's it. It's just a big ole' nasty nightmare, and any minute I'm going to wake up beside my husband who didn't cheat on me... Any second now...

I pinched my arm. "Ow."

The guy shifted and I knew he had turned his head. "Why did you do that? No, never mind. I don't want to know. Just tighten up your grip and start praying. We need a miracle."

I opened my mouth to tell him to let me down so I could get in my car and lock myself inside, but a set of headlights pulled off the main road and crept toward us.

I allowed the breath I was holding to release. My prayers had been answered. I was safe!

I moved to climb down off the guy's back, but his hands shot to my thighs and stilled me in my place.

Damn, he was strong.

"Why—"

"Shh!"

The brakes squeaked a bit as the black, late model Cadillac came to a complete stop in front of us.

The wolves had merely moved out of the way, instead of running off. They appeared to be waiting for something. I didn't have to wait long to find out what that something was.

The driver got out, popped a black umbrella open, then walked around to the opposite side of the car and opened the rear door.

The lights were shining in my eyes, and the wolves didn't seem to be a death threat at the moment, so I brought one of my hands up to shield the glare. I needed to see who was here to save us. I wanted to yell for help again, but I had a strange feeling that wouldn't be the best thing to do; I didn't want to get the attention of the wolves again; they appeared to be enamored with whomever was about to step out of the car without a care in the world that there were several hungry carnivores just waiting to rip his or her throat out. The wolves hadn't even acknowledged the driver getting out.

Were they pets? Surely not.

The guy holding me drew in a sharp breath and then swore as a figure emerged from the car. I still couldn't see any of the person's features, only that he was clearly a male, and tall.

"Let her go. It's me you want. Hurting the girl is against the laws by which we are bound. We at least hold that in common."

Laws by which we are bound?

"The woman won't be harmed," the man spoke from under the umbrella.

I gasped in horror. He'd found me!

"Marc," I whispered.

"Would you like to release my wife or would you rather my pack take her from you?"

CHAPTER 6

JAXON

Wife?

"Please tell me he's joking," Jaxon whispered over his shoulder, but he received no reply. "Were you sent to spy on me? To hunt me?" he said louder.

Still no answer.

"Say something or I will throw you in the mud! I'm sure that suit you're wearing cost enough to feed ten starving kids for a month."

"I—I—"

"Come to me, Mena. We have much to discuss, you and me," Marc said.

The girl Jaxon had brought from the bar issued from the shadows and walked to stand beside the pack leader, hooking her arm casually through his as if she was a prize he had won.

Jaxon felt Mena tense. So, Blondie had been the one to sick the dogs on him, and it appeared there was a bit of tension floating through the air between her and Mena, too.

"I don't want to go with him," Mena said in a rushed whisper by Jaxon's ear. "Yes, I am his wife, but he cheated on me and we fought and I left him. That is why I am here. It's why my eye is nearly swollen shut. I don't know you, but for some reason I trust you more than I do a man I have lived with for over twelve years. You swore you would get us out of here alive. I'm counting on you to be true to your word."

The wolves inched closer, their growls low and menacing. It wasn't his first encounter with the mutts, but it was the first time he would be protecting something besides his own hide.

Jaxon turned his head and looked into honest, pale green eyes.

He told himself he would be able to tell if she was lying, but the truth was that it really didn't matter to him if she was or not; he wanted to get out of this fight alive and take her with him.

17

Phoenix would likely remove his nuts for bringing the wife of the werewolf pack leader to their lair, but he would deal with that problem when and if it arose. Hell, who was he kidding? There would be no if; it was definitely a when.

"Let me be clear. If you're lying, I will kill you myself."

"Don't go with him, Mena. You don't know what he is. He is a danger to you, and he is my enemy."

Jaxon never took his eyes from her as the wolves slowly closed in on them. "I need your answer now."

"I won't let their kind have you, Mena. I will see you dead first, sweetheart." Marc roared through the rain, "Take her from him!"

She tightened her grip around Jaxon and closed her eyes, then whispered, "Let's go."

Jaxon had to clear a path, and he had to do it quickly or they would be at the bottom of a dog pile soon.

He spun around and kicked out with his right leg, knocking the beast closest to him into the one beside it.

Mena didn't make a sound, but her arms and legs constricted around his body almost vise-like. He smiled and reached to grab a silver dagger from the sheath on his calf, then held it up so she could grab it.

"Take this and put a hole in anything that gets too close."

She hesitated a moment before she took it from him. "But they're dogs—"

"You don't believe that any more than I do," he said dryly, and released the dagger when he was sure she had a good grip on it. There was more where that one had come from, and he retrieved a blade from his other sheath and a handgun from the shoulder holster under his jacket.

It was time to play.

Backing up wasn't an option.

Knowing there were at least four werewolves behind him, and that Mena was riding piggy, he swiftly moved forward, toward the leader and the whore who had sold him out to the werewolf pack.

They would be okay as long as Marc didn't shift, Jaxon thought, then recognized the all too familiar silver shine in the leader's eyes and knew that Mr. Hyde was about to make an appearance.

Swearing under his breath, Jaxon knew it was too late to change his tactics without getting the girl on his back killed, the one he'd sworn to that he would get them through this alive.

A brief panic rushed through him when he heard one of the beasts snap its jaws behind him, but the fear was soon laid to rest when he heard Mena let out a grunt and then a sharp yelp filled the night air.

Jaxon grinned. "You okay?"

"Yeah," she said, sounding exasperated. "I—I think I killed it."

Bringing his arm up quick, Jaxon squeezed the trigger on the glock twice and the wolf fell instantly to the muck. "Doubtful," he said, and shoved the silver blade of his dagger through the top of a wolf's skull, then pulled it out just as swiftly.

Killing those two gave him another option and opened another path. He took it, knowing Mena's husband wouldn't let him take her, at least not alive anyway. He knew the pack leader to be a cruel and strong-minded ruler, and he didn't have a clue how a woman like Mena had stayed with a man like that for over a decade.

He prayed again that she wasn't a spy.

As he put a silver bullet in the heart of one last beast in his way, he caught sight of the leader shifting and took that as his cue to get the hell out of there. He ran.

"Oh, God! What's happening to Marc?"

Jaxon didn't answer Mena's question. Letting her come to the conclusion that her husband was a werewolf on her own could possibly make it easier to understand when he told her what *he* was. He hoped. If not, at least they had the wife of the local pack leader and a very important piece of information: his true identity.

That itself was worth gold.

"He's gaining on us!" Mena yelled. "Is he going to kill us?"

Jaxon pushed his speed to the limit, even knowing giving it all he had wouldn't be enough to get them away and safe; Phoenix was the only one fast enough to outrun the pack leader.

Heavy paws pounded the broken pavement and mud behind them and Jaxon could hear the labored breathing of the monster growing nearer.

It was only a matter of seconds and they would both be goners, he thought, and handed the gun over his shoulder. It wasn't possible for him to turn and shoot Mena's husband, but maybe she could—maybe she would.

"Take the gun and shoot him, Mena! I know he is your husband, but if you don't—I won't be able to keep my promise. He will kill me and take you. You don't have to kill him—a leg would be sufficient. Aim for the shoulder."

She pushed his hand with the pistol in it away from her. "Are you crazy? I've never fired a gun before! I couldn't hit the broadside of a barn!"

"You either try or I will leave without you. How much do you want to live? Because I'm not dying for someone I just met. It's the only way you're going with me. Take the weapon, Mena."

She took it, and Jaxon half expected to see his life flash before his eyes as a bullet went through his head, but there was nothing, nothing but the sound of those thunderous paws and heavy breathing getting closer still.

What the hell is she doing? I can't keep up this pace forever.

"Shoot him!"

Jaxon's blood froze in his veins the instant Mena screamed. The gun fired and they were knocked to the ground at the same time.

CHAPTER 7

MENA

The sound of water dripping brought me out of my unconscious state, but I lay still, trying to conclude where I was and why my body felt like it had been hit by a truck. The memory of the night was a bit foggy, but I knew with all the pain I was feeling that it had not been a dream.

"Just lie still," a girl said softly. "I'm not trying to hurt you, but this may sting a little."

A scream involuntarily erupted from my throat when the girl touched my leg, as it felt like she was branding me with a hot iron. I shot upright and jerked my leg away from the young brunette.

Looking down, my eyes focused for the first time on an ugly gash down the outside of my right thigh. I knew how it had happened, but my mind refused to believe it.

I shook my head in disbelief as my hands shot up to hold back a sob.

Through my tear-filled vision, I saw the girl put a wet cloth in a bowl of pinkish water. My blood. That's all she had touched me with: a wet cloth, not a branding iron.

"My name is Lea." She didn't say anything else, just waited for me to let that small introduction soak in.

"Mena," I said with a quivering voice.

A smile stretched across her pretty face, but she didn't reach for the cloth. It was clear she was giving me the time I needed to trust her.

Relaxing a little, I scooted toward her and straightened my leg out, giving her silent permission to clean the wound.

"I'm sorry—"

She shook her head. "The fault is mine. I should have at least put some numbing spray on that bite before trying to clean it. I wasn't thinking. Jaxon will be furious—"

"Wait—what did you say?"

"There's a numbing medicine I can put on it, so it won't hurt you as I clean it. You may feel a little discomfort, but it should at least be bearable—"

"No, you said it is a bite," I snapped, and then shrank back, ashamed of my outburst at the sweet girl.

She only sat on the stool and looked at me with kind but sorrowful eyes.

I swallowed hard. "What bit me?" I whispered, my eyes stinging with fresh, hot tears and dreading what she would say.

She averted eye contact with me and stood quickly. "I'm going to go get that numbing spray and some ibuprofen. It'll help with the pain—"

"Tell me, please." I pleaded with words and my eyes when I grabbed her hand and she was forced to look at me again.

She sighed. "I'll send Jaxon in to talk with you when he's through speaking with Phoenix. I'm not sure how much I'm allowed to tell you. The wait shouldn't be long. I'll be back soon to help you get cleaned up and dress your wounds." Her gaze fell before she turned toward the door to leave. "You will heal quickly, so we need to get the dirt out."

She left me in the room alone.

Sitting there waiting to find out what had happened to me was driving me out of my mind.

Jaxon.

Was that the guy who had saved me? Had he survived? Had the horrible thing Marc turned into let him live? Or had he killed my husband?

I was surprised to realize that it wouldn't have bothered me in the least if someone had answered the last question with a yes.

One thing was certain: I couldn't sit in this room and wait any longer.

Wincing as a sharp pain shot up my leg, I placed my foot on the cement floor and limped toward the door.

There was no sound coming from the other side as I put my ear to the door to listen, so I took in a shaky breath and tried the knob. It turned freely in my hand and I opened the door to find a dark hallway.

The walls were made of gray stone and the air was cool. It seemed like I was underground, as I saw no sign of natural light to state otherwise. There hadn't been any windows in the room they had put me in, so the guess was an uneducated one still.

Raised voices came from my right and my head shot around to see a faint glow at the end of the hall.

After taking a few steps in the direction of the heated argument, I discovered a door was ajar and that was where the voices had issued from.

"Why can't you see what an asset she is to us?" a male voice said, and after peeking through the gap between the door and the jamb, I realized it belonged to the guy who had gotten me away from Marc. He had lived and followed through on his promise.

I felt a sense of relief rush over me. Then another male spoke.

"She is a danger to us if she lives, Jaxon, and you know it—"

"Not if you turn her before her first change tonight. The moon will be at its fullest this night and we will have missed our chance to make her hybrid—"

My hand shot up to stifle a gasp and both males' heads turned swiftly to look toward the door. My feet shuffled back and I bumped into the wall behind me, and then I turned and ran. I had to get out of there. I still didn't know what had happened to me, but what the two men were plotting didn't sound like anything I would be interested in: death or turning me into one of those beasts I had seen Marc turn into.

This isn't real! I tried to force my mind to accept it, but my pounding heart beating against my ribcage and my bare feet slapping the cold concrete with each step I ran suggested otherwise. *This isn't real! This isn't real! This isn't real!*

Jaxon was suddenly in front of me and I slammed into his hard body. He wrapped me in his arms and I struggled to break free of his hold, but he was so strong.

I screamed, "This isn't real!"

CHAPTER 8

JAXON

Mena, it's me," Jaxon said. "I won't hurt you. Calm down."

"Let me go!" Mena screamed. "You're not turning me into one of those—those *things* that Marc is." She jerked away and he let her go. She stared at him as she tried to catch her breath. "Why would you want to turn me into one of them?" Her lower lip trembled. "And how—*how* is that even possible?" she yelled, but Jaxon didn't speak. She wouldn't be ready to listen to anything he had to say until she calmed down a lot.

Mena turned her head to look back down the hallway, and then in the other direction. "How do I get out of here? I need to leave this place."

"You can't leave," Phoenix's sultry voice said from behind Mena, and her head whipped around in surprise. It was clear she was questioning why she hadn't seen anyone where the male stood now, so close to her.

Jaxon and Mena both stiffened as Phoenix's long fingers came up to caress Mena's cheek. "Don't—" he started.

Ice blue eyes turned slowly to glare at Jaxon, cutting his sentence short, but Phoenix never removed his hand from Mena's face. "She is a pretty little thing, isn't she, Jaxon?"

Jaxon hesitated only a moment. "Y—yes, Master."

Phoenix nodded once and pursed his lips together into a thin line, as if contemplating what to do next. Looking back to Mena, he said, "I'm sure you have questions. I swear nothing will happen to you until after you have made your decision."

"My—my decision?" Mena stuttered out.

Phoenix simply removed his hand from her face and held it out in the direction of his quarters.

MENA

"Have a seat, Mena," the man said.

He was one of the most attractive men I had ever seen in my life. Wavy, chestnut hair fell nearly to his shoulders and loose curls framed his face. His intense eyes, that seemed to bore through to my very soul, were the color of ice glaciers. Against the light bronze color of his skin, they appeared to glow as they studied me.

I tried not to stare at him, but it was quite difficult not to with what he was wearing, or rather what he wasn't wearing. Broad shoulders complemented a well-defined, shirtless chest. His sculpted torso was lean and would put any male model that I had ever seen to shame. The faded blue jeans he wore fit him extremely well and his feet were bare. There was nothing feminine about him, but he was so handsome he was pretty. An Adonis reincarnated perhaps.

The clearing of a throat snapped me out of admiring my captor, and I glanced over to see Jaxon with his hand held out to a couch. He raised an eyebrow nervously, and I looked back to the other male. He was waiting for me to obey him; that was clear now. When he'd offered me a seat, he had actually given me an order to sit down, his seductive voice only making it sound like he was giving me an option.

I inhaled deeply as I sat on the edge of the cushion.

The corner of Adonis' mouth twitched in amusement. I found that irritated me profusely, but I wasn't sure if it was my anger or the lust that he was stirring in me that caused me so much agitation.

My hands curled into tight fists on my lap to keep from fanning my blouse. It was hot in the room all of a sudden.

"My name is Phoenix. I hear you've met Jaxon. He informed me of what occurred with the werewolf leader and his pack—"

Despite how much I wanted to cry, I laughed instead. "Werewolf?"

Phoenix's eyes darted to Jaxon. "I thought you said she knew."

"She saw him change. It doesn't mean her mind accepts it. She's in denial."

"Wait, you're saying that werewolves are real, and that a man I have been married to for over twelve years is one of them?" I said, and didn't feel like laughing anymore. I actually felt a little dizzy.

The two men stared at one another for a long moment before Phoenix looked back to me. "Not just a werewolf, Mena, but *the* werewolf. He was the pack leader. We've been trying to discover his true identity for over a decade, so we could ruin him publicly, but he covered his tracks well."

I sat there and tried to process what they were telling me, that my husband turns into a monster once a month. They didn't look crazy, but they sure sounded like it. I shook my head. Werewolves weren't real. But if they weren't, then what the hell had Marc turned into?

I locked eyes with Jaxon and remembered an earlier question I had asked him that had gone unanswered. "Why would you want to turn me into one of them?"

He wasn't the one who answered.

"You already are one of them," Phoenix said, and I reached out and grabbed the arm of the couch to steady my swaying body. "Actually, you are now *the* one, Mena. You became one of them the moment your husband bit you, and you became the pack leader a second later when you put a silver bullet through his heart. To become a pack leader, you have to take the life of the current one."

I couldn't breathe.

CHAPTER 9

PHOENIX

The girl intrigued him. That was a fact, perhaps even more so than any other female he had ever met before. And that was saying a lot for this one.

Jaxon had been right: she was enchanting, but Phoenix had killed plenty of beautiful women, as well as not, in his long life. Her being the new werewolf pack leader only made him want to drain her of the enemy blood that much more.

Was he toying with her? Maybe. Mayhap it was the way Jaxon had begged him to spare her life that kept him from breaking her neck then and there. Could be. Jaxon had never really asked him for anything, which was why he still held second in command status.

The guy had said it was his fault entirely the girl had been bitten in the first place, but Phoenix knew that to be untrue. He was the only one in the area strong and fast enough to take on the pack leader. And that's when Phoenix realized why the girl's heart was still beating: she was a human girl—the wife of the pack leader no less—and she did something he himself had been unable to do since the male had defeated the previous pack leader: kill him.

She couldn't stay here, he decided. She belonged with her pack. Their leader belonged with the mutts. Of course, if they returned her to them like she was now, they would see how weak she was and she would be dead before her first change.

The thought angered him, and he grew even more pissed because it had. She was a werewolf; why should he care if the beast was killed?

Disgusted with himself, Phoenix turned away from them to give the girl privacy while Jaxon consoled her.

The least he could do was get her cleaned up and fill her stomach while her humanity was still intact.

After making a quick call, Phoenix placed his cell phone on the bar and just watched her. It was obvious Jaxon was enamored with the girl—any fool could see that—and if he turned her into a hybrid—as Jaxon suggested he do—the girl would be sired to him and he would rule over two-thirds of the underworld. It wasn't the worst idea Jaxon had ever come up with; it was actually a pretty damn good one, but Phoenix knew what would happen to him if he sired her. He wouldn't be able to let Jaxon have her, because he would want her.

Phoenix shook his head at the thought. *No, I will not share my throne with anyone.*

MENA

A soft knock at the door made me jump to my feet in alarm.

Something was seriously wrong with my body. I had never moved so fast before, and the achiness I had felt after waking earlier was almost gone. My eyes widened in stunned disbelief as I glanced down at the wound where Marc had bit me. The dried blood was still all over the tattered material of my pants, but there were only faint pink lines where the injury had been.

My focus shot back to the door when the knock sounded again and a low growl echoed throughout the room. I gasped and slapped a hand over my mouth when I realized it was me who had done it.

Jaxon cautiously took my hand and helped me to sit back down on the couch. "Calm down, Mena. It's just—"

"Enter," Phoenix said, as if my behavior was normal for him, or maybe he had been expecting it. Well, I hadn't been expecting it, and it was definitely *not* normal for me to go around growling at sudden sounds.

"Oh, God," I said, and began to tremble. "I'm a dog."

"Shh… It's okay—" Jaxon tried again to comfort me, but I didn't need comforting; I needed freaking answers… and a cure!

I shot to my feet again and hurriedly put some distance between us. I warned him with my eyes to stay away.

30

He was either smart or scared, because he only stood there with his palms up. His stance was defensive, so I didn't feel threatened by him. Taking in a deep breath, I relaxed a little, but didn't go back to sit beside him. I wasn't ready for that just yet. I didn't know if I ever would be. I could tell he was doing everything in his power to try to make me comfortable, but his gestures were having the opposite effect on me.

"Sit them on the table. Thank you. You may go," Phoenix said, and I looked over to him in time to see the girl I had awoken to earlier closing the door behind her as she left the chambers.

There was no expression on Phoenix's face when I looked back at him.

"I had a hot meal and dry, warm clothing brought in. Eat while the food is still warm, and you can use my lavatory to clean yourself afterward." Phoenix lowered his head and his brow furrowed in what appeared to be confusion or thought. I only stared at him. Slowly taking the back of the chair in his hand, he pulled it out from the table and gestured with his other hand for me to take the seat. "The steak is not poisoned. However you preferred your meat before, I think you will discover rare to be your preference now." My nose scrunched up in distaste, and he grinned. "I swore no harm would come to you until after you made your decision, Mena. Please eat something."

I still didn't know what decision it was that I had to make, but an amazing scent came from the plate and I didn't care about anything in that moment except eating. My stomach rumbled and my feet involuntarily moved to the table.

CHAPTER 10

PHOENIX

He waited until he heard the bathroom door click shut before turning to Jaxon.

"I think you need to leave."

Jaxon's eyes widened. "But why? Mena needs me here—"

"She does not need you now, nor will she need you in the future. She is the queen of a werewolf pack, Jaxon—"

"You can make her hybrid and rule over—"

"Do not interrupt me again!" Phoenix thundered, and Jaxon fell to one knee and bowed his head.

"My apologies, Master, but I think—"

"You think," Phoenix spat. "Your thinking is going to get you killed! I will share my throne with no one," he finished quietly.

Jaxon waited a moment to make sure he wouldn't make the mistake of disrupting Phoenix again. "Why would you have to share your throne with anyone? You will own her and rule over the werewolves as well as the vampires."

Phoenix nodded. "That may be true, but there is one tiny detail you are forgetting."

Jaxon's eyes closed as he exhaled. "The bond."

"Yes. The bond. I refuse to make myself vulnerable—"

Jaxon's head shot up. "I can do it. Surely I've lived long enough—" His words were suddenly cut off as Phoenix's fist connected with his jaw. The punch knocked him back ten yards into the wall. A few shards of stone fell as Jaxon's body crumpled to the floor.

"Even if you were strong enough to make her hybrid, do you think I would actually let you live and become my equal as pack leader over werewolves? She is a werewolf. You are a vampire. Enemies, Jaxon. Immortal enemies. The two are not meant to bond. She's better off dead, but, if she cooperates, I will let her own pack do it and save me the trouble.

Like you said: it's entirely your fault she was bitten, right? We'll just let them fight over who will be their next leader."

Jaxon swallowed hard, and Phoenix could tell he was still trying to figure out a way the two of them could be together.

"You will not be with her. I forbid it. Now, leave my quarters while I talk with her. I don't want your interference if she disagrees with me."

Jaxon got to his feet and wiped the stone dust from his clothing. "And if she disagrees with you, what will you do?"

Phoenix contemplated his options, but quickly came to only one. "Kill her."

MENA

Like Phoenix's living chambers, his bathroom was exquisite. Everything was top notch fixtures and furnishings that had to have been shipped to him from overseas. The style was unique to say the least. I wondered if he had decorated everything himself or if his wife had done it.

I couldn't imagine what a man like him would do for a living, and then it occurred to me that he might actually be a model. I hadn't ever seen him before, but that wasn't saying much; I rarely had time to look at magazines or keep up with *Runway*. I gasped and then giggled as the thought of him being a porn star came to mind. I shook my head at the ridiculous thought; he seemed to have more respect for that beautiful body of his than to do something like that. I honestly couldn't imagine him working for anyone but himself. The whole taking orders from anyone didn't suit him. What if he was a hit man? I wondered. But what would a hit man know about werewolves? And Jaxon was so strong and fast, but nobody would be able to tell it by simply looking at him. Were they even human?

Besides the strength and speed, Jaxon looked like a fairly normal guy, but Phoenix... A sigh escaped my lips as I remembered the image of him standing in front of me with those ice cold eyes. Phoenix was anything but normal, I concluded.

I quickly towel-dried my hair, then unzipped the duffle bag Lea had packed for me. My jaw dropped. No! I gasped in horror. This had to be a mistake. I reached in and pulled out the black leather pants, holding them at arm's length so I could get a good mental picture of what a disaster the rest of my night was going to be. I groaned and tossed them on the vanity, dreading what shirt Lea thought would complete the outfit. After reaching in, I pulled out a new matching set of lacy underwear in nude, a white tank top, socks, a black fitted leather jacket and a pair of black boots with a low heel—everything was exactly my size. Lea had looked smaller than me, so I didn't have a clue whose clothes I was borrowing. She had even brought a small bag of hygiene items, including: a toothbrush, brush, face moisturizer and deodorant. I made a mental note to thank her later for *those* items.

After dressing and cleaning up after myself, I looked in the mirror and huffed. "That's enough stalling, Biker Chick. You aren't going to find the answers to your problems in the john."

I turned the handle and opened the bathroom door to hear Phoenix shouting, but the instant I walked into the room, all fell silent.

My eyes met Jaxon's. He looked nervous as he glanced back to Phoenix.

"I'm begging you…" Jaxon said, and let the rest of his sentence go unsaid.

"Get out," Phoenix said, his tone gruff.

Jaxon's sad eyes shifted back to me for only a moment, before he turned and walked from the room, slamming the door in his wake.

Phoenix stood with his back to me, anger radiating from his rigid posture.

"What was that all about?" I said quietly.

Instead of answering me, he crossed the room and filled a crystal glass with a dark liquid.

I lay the bag with my soiled clothing in it on the floor, not wanting to get any mud from last night's adventure on the furniture.

"You know, usually Twenty Questions is played with one person asking the questions and the other person answering them. I overheard you talking with Jaxon earlier about how I would go through my first change tonight, so I'm guessing we don't have a lot of time to strategize a plan to keep that from happening."

Phoenix raised the glass to his lips and took a sip, but before he set it back down he opened his mouth to speak and then turned those bright, light blue eyes on me. No words came out. He just looked at me, with absolutely no expression on that beautiful face to let me know what was going through that mysterious mind of his.

"There is no way to keep it from happening," he finally said, and then downed the remains of what was in the glass in one huge gulp. "There is no reversing lycanthropy," he finished, and placed the glass back on the bar.

I had figured as much, which was why I probably hadn't freaked out yet. Either that or I was still in shock. Being this calm about everything I'd been through in the last twelve hours or so was beginning to scare me a little.

I didn't flinch away as he continued to stare, not even when he let his eyes roam down, then back up my body for the second time. I told myself he was just making sure Lea had followed through on his orders and brought me everything I needed, and that it had nothing to do with how silly I looked in tight leather pants. I had caught Jaxon looking at me in a similar way, but him staring at me didn't make all the heat in my body rush to my face the way that Phoenix's eyes on me did.

Answers, Mena. You need answers. "What about you? What are you?"

Phoenix smiled then, and I immediately locked my knees to keep them from buckling under my weight.

"I'm your enemy, Mena."

My voice was shaky as he slowly walked toward me. Actually, stalked would be a more appropriate way of explaining how he closed the distance between us. "Y—you don't have to be my enemy. I—I am pretty easy to get along with."

Running from him had already been proven to be a mistake, so I remained where I stood.

He shook his head slowly. "That's not the way it is between your kind and mine," he said, his voice floating through those sultry lips in a seductive whisper.

I swallowed as he made his way around behind me, but I could feel him, and he was so close. "Why?" I said, my voice cracking under the intensity of his presence.

His breath tickled my neck as the words left his mouth. "Because I am a vampire."

Faster than I had ever moved before, I turned in a flash and fell into a fighting stance, a low growl erupting from my chest as our eyes locked together.

"See," he said calmly, as if he had expected what I would do before it even happened. "Your instincts are taking over. You were made to hate me, just as I was made to hate you."

I didn't hate him. My body and mind were going through changes I didn't understand, but I knew I didn't hate him.

Phoenix still hadn't moved, so I relaxed a little.

His eyebrows raised in interest. "You do not wish to fight me anymore?" he said, his tone implying his surprise.

"I never wanted to fight you. I was simply going to defend myself if you decided to attack me. And—and I don't hate you. That's just absurd. Whatever I've become won't change who I am. I don't go around hating people just because I can, so until you give me a better reason other than that you are a vampire," I shrugged, "I guess we can get matching BFF bracelets."

He blinked at me a few times, and I grinned, extremely pleased with myself for throwing a kink in his plan to intimidate me.

"BFF?" he said, and one of his eyebrows popped up.

My smile grew. "You know, best friends forever?"

He rubbed his hands over his face, but snickered lightly as he did so. "You want to be my friend, do you? That's definitely a first."

I shrugged. "Well, I don't want to be enemies."

A sudden heat flashed in his eyes as a low growl vibrated from his chest, and I realized he had taken my statement to mean I wanted to be his lover. I blushed again. I hadn't really meant it to come out like it did.

Phoenix startled me when he started toward the door. "Come with me," he ordered.

"What? Why? Where are we going?" I was almost jogging to keep up with his long, quick strides.

"You have to leave."

"What? Why?"

"Stop asking questions," he said shortly.

"But I need to know what to do!"

"Stop talking, woman," he growled.

"Won't they look for me—and try to kill me? What does Jaxon think I should—"

Phoenix stopped suddenly and threw me against a wall, his hard body pinning mine to the cool stone. One of his hands gripped my wrist and trapped it above my head as the fingers of his other hand shot into my hair and grabbed the back of my head before it could slam against the rock.

It all happened so fast. His breathing was labored, as was mine, but I didn't feel threatened. The fight was gone out of him and the anger had quickly been replaced with a hunger that was foreign to me. I couldn't tell if it was sex or my blood that he wanted.

He leaned closer, breathing in the scent of his soap on my skin.

"You… have… to leave here."

I could feel his warm breath on my face as he moved his head back to look down at me, and I could see in his eyes that he wanted to close the gap between our lips as much as I wanted him to.

"Why?" I whispered again.

"Because, if you stay, I will make you mine. You will belong to me. I will do as Jaxon suggests and sire you, making me ruler over the werewolves as well as the vampires. You and I would be bonded together for an eternity, Mena, but I share my throne with no one." His gaze fell from my eyes to my lips. "You are dangerous to me," he said softly, "because for you, I almost would."

He released me then turned and walked into a room full of weapons.

I stumbled a little as the weight of him left my body.

Well, that answered my unspoken question of whether he was married or not.

CHAPTER 11

PHOENIX

As Phoenix stormed away from Mena, he found the simple task of putting one foot in front of the other the greatest challenge he had ever encountered.

She was just a woman, a woman that should, by everything he had ever believed, be his enemy, so why did he want to, all of a sudden, give it all up for—for what? It wasn't like they could have some sort of relationship. Her pack—if they didn't kill her—wouldn't allow that to happen, and Phoenix refused to think what his clan would say or do.

It was foolish of him to even contemplate what could happen, because it never would. It didn't mean he didn't want it to, though, because he did; with every ounce of his damned soul, he wanted to rush back to where he had left her and make her his.

Forcing himself into focus, Phoenix grabbed at silver throwing blades and daggers on the wall in front of him, placing them on the stainless table in the center of the room, before going to the other side to retrieve guns and ammo.

He knew the instant Mena looked at him; he could feel her green eyes on him. She was curious, he knew, but she didn't seem afraid. She should be. He should have been stronger and made her fear him. He had been doing a damn good job of intimidating her until he'd seen her in leather, then he had all but fallen at her feet like a love-struck fool.

Lea would pay greatly for doing that to him.

"Are we going to war?" Mena asked quietly. "Or are you planning to use those on me?"

Holsters. Holsters.

Phoenix walked to a cabinet and opened it to holsters, sheaths and a ton of other miscellaneous items needed to prepare one for battle.

"Phoenix?" she whispered, stopping him in his tracks.

His eyes slammed shut and in he breathed the scent of her as she slowly entered the room. Clearing his throat and scrambling in his mind to lock up his sanity before she had complete and utter control over him, he opened his eyes, cool and collected once again, and glared at her under dark lashes. "You're going to need protection from your own kind until they accept you as their pack leader. I have a feeling none of them are going to like having a woman as their Alpha."

"And you're just going to put all that stuff on me and throw me to the wolves, so to speak?"

His lips thinned as he pursed them together, and he nodded once. "Yes. That about sums it up," he said, and had to turn back to the cabinet to keep from seeing the sadness in her eyes.

She already knew she was a dead dog. Why sugarcoat it for her?

"Do you want this war to end, between werewolves and vampires?"

Phoenix watched his knuckles turn white as he squeezed the leather holster in his fist. "It's not that easy—"

"I didn't say it would be easy, but I do believe it's possible."

He turned then to look at her. How had she become so strong in so little time? He remembered when he had become master of his vampire clan. He'd been terrified. You didn't have anyone to look up to when you were at the top. Nothing to gain and everything to lose. He knew how she felt. Alone. He had felt alone. He still felt that way, but now there was Mena, perhaps offering him another option.

"You want me to make you hybrid?"

She shook her head. "No. I don't want to belong to anyone."

"What do you suggest we do?"

She smiled. "We try."

MENA

The expression etched on his face was comical to me. Had I suggested we do something that absurd? I didn't think so.

I watched him, waiting patiently for him to come to a conclusion. Would he think that working together to end something so horrible was a bad thing? I knew I couldn't do it alone. I wasn't even sure I could survive against my own people, much less end a war that had been going on for God only knew how long.

We were both leaders and it was up to us what happened, right? How was it that he couldn't comprehend how simple it should be to stop all this crap? Sure, we would have to convince a lot of our own that this was the right thing to do, but, honestly, what were we even fighting for? More gain? More power? Bragging rights? I just didn't see it. Maybe it was just me.

"Let me get this straight: you want us to be friends and work together to end a war that has lasted over a thousand years? That *is* what you're saying, right?"

I shrugged. "Why not?"

His eyebrows raised a fraction and were hidden behind the loose curls hanging almost to his eyes. "I think it's a death sentence for both of us."

"So, you would rather be my enemy?"

He let his eyes slowly sweep down and then back up my body again. After a moment, he shook his head. "No—no, I don't want to be your enemy."

My heart swelled. Maybe this could work, that was if I could survive being slaughtered by my own pack tonight. I wasn't looking forward to meeting them, but the inevitable was going to happen when the moon rose high in the sky. I couldn't stay here with Phoenix; I had no idea what I would be capable of after I turned into a werewolf. He had been right: our kind were made to be enemies and hate each other, fight to the death. My goal was to change that.

"I was hoping you'd say that." I looked to the table and the weapons he had put there for me to use to protect myself against my own people. "Load me up. I have respect to earn tonight."

CHAPTER 12

PHOENIX

Mena looked like a true, badass warrior after Phoenix put the last sheath in place on her right thigh.

Stepping back a bit, his fingers came up to play along his chin in thought. There was something missing, he mused, and then took his cell from his pocket and texted Lea a message.

"Well?"

"Something's missing," he said. "Lea is on her way."

Mena snickered. "I don't think anything else is going to fit on my body."

Phoenix's mouth turned up at one corner as he thought about how fun it would be to take everything back off and not stop at the clothes once he got to them.

Mena looked to the door when Lea entered with a brush and ponytail holders, but Phoenix kept his eyes on her as his assistant went to work.

He nodded once, silently dismissing Lea after she finished. She left quietly.

"How do I look?"

Sin. A good nightmare. Sexy as hell. The death of me. My ruin. He cleared his throat and walked to the cabinet to put the things he hadn't used away. "You look fine," he mumbled.

"I look like Lara Croft."

"Who is Lara—" Phoenix started, but turned around to find her right in front of him, and all of a sudden his vocals forgot how to work.

"Am I ready?"

"No. Not even close." He walked around her and out of the room. She followed. He could feel her and sense the questions coming. "Lea, is the car ready?"

"It is," Lea said, and fell into step beside him.

"The car?" Mena said.

Lea handed Phoenix a strip of black fabric without answering Mena

"And you know where to take her?"

"Yes, Master."

"Take me where?"

"Good. Give her an untraceable cell and put my number in her contacts in case she needs backup."

Lea nodded and handed the phone in her hand to Mena.

"But where am I going?" Mena said as they arrived at a staircase, leading up to a single door.

Phoenix reached back and took Mena's hand without giving her eye contact. "What's the time?"

"6:10," Lea replied. "The sun set twenty-three minutes ago."

Phoenix nodded and tried to ignore the tingling sensation he was getting from touching Mena's bare skin. "Good," he said, and unlocked and then opened the door at the top of the stairs. He made brief eye contact with Lea after she issued from the basement after Mena.

"I'll wait in the car," Lea said, and then left them to be alone.

"Phoenix—"

"Shh…" he said, and turned to face her. Why had he thought the urge to kiss her would have simply just vanished in the minute and a half it took to get away from her in the weapon room? If anything, it had only grown stronger. Was he crazy to let her walk out of there without protection from his clan? The pack would kill her. He knew they would. If for some reason he was wrong about that, there was the other worry in the back of his mind: the men. There were so many for her to choose from. Which one would she choose to mate with? Which one would he have to kill? And why did he feel like he needed to stake his claim on her, mark *his* territory?

Those green eyes looked up at him, frightened. She was so scared. He could hear the rapid beating of her heart and see it pulse in the light blue vein of her jugular.

Phoenix fought the impulse to let his fangs fully extend as her scent wafted past his nose. He knew she had wanted him to kiss her earlier, almost as much as he had wanted to, but that would have only caused them bigger, more dangerous problems.

Werewolves and vampires are not meant to bond, he told himself, yet again.

"You will be fine," he lied. "Take out the biggest one first. It will let them know you are serious, and maybe they will back off."

Mena nodded and tears filled those beautiful eyes.

44

Christ! She was going to be his undoing!

He shook her a little. "You have to be strong. They can smell your fear. If you can make it through this first change without them killing you, you'll be fine. You took the life of the pack leader, Mena, so you have more power than they do. I wish we had time to discover all the abilities you have, but sadly, the moon is rising and you'll change soon. I don't want to be anywhere near you when that happens."

Her breath hitched and he struggled to keep from comforting her; it would only cause her to fall apart, and focused and strong was what she needed to be at the moment.

"I will be expecting your call in the morning. Stay alive and make that happen, Mena." He took a step back and held out his hand to lead her to the car, but she flung herself on him and wrapped her arms around his torso. His reaction was instantaneous. His arms enveloped her and held her shuddering form tightly in his embrace.

How could he do this? How could he just let her go in alone?

"Stay," he heard himself whisper. He moved back enough so he could frame her face in his hands. "I know it sounds cruel, but I have a cell I can lock you in until you change back. We need more time to sort this out before you go to them."

Mena gave him a sad smile and shook her head. "I need to do this now. I will look weak to them if I hide. I can do this, Phoenix."

"I'll come with you and bring some of my clan as backup—" he started, but she was shaking her head again, refusing his offer to help.

"We are trying to stop this war. If you or any of your people show up, I fear it will only enrage them. I haven't even met them yet, but I can somehow feel them in me. They are waiting."

Phoenix sighed and pulled her to him once again. "You have my number. I will be there with an army the moment you call. Well, as long as it's still night. The sun and I don't exactly see eye to eye on a few things, well, actually just one thing."

Mena snickered and pulled out of the embrace.

"You are not alone in this." He brushed the back of his fingers over her cheek and sighed, knowing he needed to pull away and put some distance between them. How had he fallen under her spell so easily?

"I will call if I need you," she said and backed away.

With an ache in his chest he was unfamiliar with, he let her go.

"I'll walk you to the car." Phoenix turned on his heel and strode to the door. It felt like he had a thousand pound weight on his arm as he lifted it to put his hand on the door handle. He had to let her go. She could change at any minute.

Mena cleared her throat from behind him, and he turned the handle and opened the door a few inches, and then shut it with a slam and turned to her wide eyes.

He didn't give himself time to talk his way out of it; he just took her face in his hands and brought her mouth up to meet his.

There was a short surprised sound that came from her, but it quickly turned into a low moan of approval and her lips parted, inviting him in. He didn't need any more encouragement than that. He took. Greedily. Without remorse. He was sure she would probably feel regret later. He didn't care. This was now. And that was all that mattered to him.

His hands slid back behind her head and he pulled the long braid Lea had constructed and broke away from her mouth to take possession of her neck. Even though his fangs protruded slightly, he didn't strike her. Blood wasn't what he wanted from her. He wanted her body, blissfully naked, on his bed and spread out for the taking.

He kissed over her collarbone and made his way back to her mouth, knowing full well that his fantasy wasn't going to happen this night, nor would he even try if they hadn't been faced with the cruel reality that she would turn into a wolf and howl at the moon in only a few short hours. Minutes. Seconds. Who the hell cared when it would actually happen? The fact was that it would happen, and a lot sooner than he wanted it to.

"You have put a spell on me, wolf. Each second that passes that I don't have your mouth on mine is sweet, agonizing torture. Give me your lips."

"Come get them, bloodsucker," she said in a husky whisper, and man, didn't that make him want to risk Father Time and the beast that was sure to come.

He quickly turned them around and shoved her against the door with his body, his thick erection pushing against her pelvis, seeking access and being denied by the denim of his jeans and the slick leather of her pants.

She cried out in pleasure and wrapped her arms around his neck, pulling him down to claim her mouth once again.

A soft knock came from the door he had Mena's body pressed against, but Phoenix ignored it as he devoured her sweet, supple lips. The nipping, teasing and tongue tango was cut short when the knock came again, loud and furiously demanding his attention.

Damn it, Lea!

"What?" he barked, and pulled Mena closer as she nuzzled and kissed his neck. His damn head was completely clouded with lust for this woman. What day was it again? Oh, right. Full moon! Son of a bitch!

"Master, I think Mena's pack is coming to get her. There are a lot of howls going on out here and they seem to be getting closer."

Phoenix sighed hard and slapped the door with his palm.

Mena stood up straight and he took a step back from her so she could adjust her clothing.

"I have to go. They can sense where I am and they will find you and your clan. I don't want to put you in jeopardy."

"We can handle them, Mena."

"Still, I don't want any bloodshed if I can prevent it from happening. Your clan of vampires aren't the only ones I'm worried about. The pack might not have accepted me as their leader yet, but they are my pack and I intend to protect them the best I can. They will see reason, Phoenix. Give them time." She reached up to touch his face when he placed his hands on his hips and looked away. "Believe me. I wouldn't ask you to choose between your clan and me, so don't expect me to just side with you when our families have their differences. It will all .work out in the end. You'll see."

"Master," Lea said again.

Mena rose up on her toes and kissed him tenderly on the lips. "I'll call you in the morning—"

"Come to me," he demanded. "I need to see that they haven't harmed you in any way."

She shook her head and took the black strip of fabric from his pocket. "I'll see you soon, Phoenix."

Mena turned and opened the door then handed Lea the material so that she could be blindfolded.

Phoenix watched Lea drive her away with his jaw clenched and his fingers curled into tight fists at his side. Patience wasn't something he was good at.

"You let her go?" Jaxon's voice came from behind him, and Phoenix turned to glare at the male.

"Get a dozen men together. We're going after her. Make sure they are all aware that if anyone hurts her, they will answer to my wrath."

CHAPTER 13

MENA

Pitch. Black. There was no light getting through this sucker, but even though I couldn't see anything as Lea drove me away from Phoenix, my other senses had heightened and I knew exactly where I was.

That didn't make me feel good. I mean, if I knew how to get back to the Master Vampire of the city, then my new pack wouldn't stop interrogating and torturing me until I told them his location or they killed me.

Damn the choices.

I could feel their presence all around me. Curiosity was the emotion I was picking up most, so I felt relatively safe still. Although, I knew that could change at any given moment. I wasn't naïve to believe otherwise.

"Lea, you can pull over here."

The beat of her heart escalated, and I suppose it was the first time I realized that I could hear it… and that it pumped blood through her veins. What was a human doing as a Master Vampire assistant?

"Phoenix gave me strict orders to—"

I reached up and ripped the cloth from my eyes, meeting brown frightened ones in the rearview mirror. "Tell Phoenix to take it up with me or that I put a gun to your head, whichever you think would be more convincing to him, but you need to stop this car and let me out before my pack stops it for you. They're here."

Lea jerked the wheel and the car came to a stop on the shoulder of the two-lane road.

I glanced out the window at the dark woods. It unsettled me a bit, how they felt like home to me. I grabbed for the handle—

"Wait," Lea said, turning in her seat so she could look back at me. There was still a faint glow from the setting sun on the horizon, but I was betting she couldn't see me as clearly as I could see her; my night vision was impressive.

"If you don't call Phoenix, he will come looking for you. I've never seen him act this way about anyone before. You mean something to him and... he protects things that are important to him. Don't get yourself killed or this war will have seemed like a battle up until now."

"Tell Phoenix to keep his shirt on. I'm a big girl." I grabbed for the handle and opened the door.

"Uh... Mena?"

With a huff, my head whipped around to her, but she was looking out the windshield. My gaze shifted to see more than twenty men in the high beams. Phoenix was standing in the center of the frontline.

"Tell him yourself. I guess he decided not to wait for your call after all."

This had disaster written all over it. What the hell was he thinking?

"Get out of here, Lea. This is going to get ugly and I don't want you in the middle of it."

She nodded vigorously and shoved the car in drive. I jumped out and slammed the door just as she punched the gas, doing a U-turn and leaving me to face a vampire clan and a pack of werewolves on my own.

If I survived this night, Karma and I were going to have a serious talk when the sun came up.

The bright silver glow of the moon shone down, spotlighting Phoenix and his men. His jaw was clenched tight and his eyes were intense as they glared at me, daring me to disagree with his decision.

I shook my head. "You shouldn't have come here."

"I'll ask forgiveness in the morning."

A long howl cut through the night's stillness and my eyes drifted closed as a shivering feeling of a foreign power caressed my skin. The moon was asking me to accept it as my own, to assume ownership of my freak change in fate.

I could feel the beast in me stretching its long legs. She would make her appearance soon.

A low growl reverberated from my chest and my knees buckled under the pressure.

"Mena!" Jaxon shouted, and my head shot up to see Phoenix had the male held back with one of his arms.

Had Jaxon lost his mind? "Get him out of here!" I roared, and another howl echoed through the air, forcing me to drop to my palms on the pavement.

Two more howls bellowed from the shadows of the forest and I screamed out as the pain consumed me. They were calling for her. They were calling my beast out.

Through tear-filled eyes, I looked up to meet Phoenix's stare.

"Accept it, Mena. Let her free," he said, and then a choir of howls bellowed throughout the night, knocking me flat to the asphalt.

I writhed and seizured uncontrollably, the unyielding pavement scraping against the flesh of my face and hands.

"Claim it, Mena!" Phoenix shouted.

I rolled to my side and my eyes fluttered open to see the moon, shining magnificently down on me. In that moment it was all so clear to me what I had to do. Phoenix was right. I knew then he hadn't brought his clan here to start a brawl with my new family. He wanted to make sure I knew I wasn't alone, that he would be there for me in anything I went through, even if it meant putting his own life on the line.

A sense of peace washed over me and I nodded to the moon. "I accept you."

I could feel the beast in me. We were one and the same. She had her own thoughts and intentions, but in the end, *we* were one. She was me and I was her. We both seemed to be content with that.

"Mena?" Phoenix's voice was low and confusion was clear in his tone.

Lifting my head, I realized the pain was gone. My wolf was still there, but she hadn't forced herself out. She knew me, because she was me, and we were both conscious of the fact that this war between the vampires and werewolves would not end unless changes and new laws were put in place. I assumed she was leaving this one up to me. Though, I had no doubts she would have her say about things to come.

Hmmm... I wondered what she thought about Phoenix.

I got to my hands and knees, and then stood and wiped at the dirt and tiny pebbles embedded in my leather clothing. I was sure glad my wolf had decided to wait for her grand introduction. I was just beginning to like the clothes, or maybe it was the way Phoenix looked at me when I wore them that I liked best.

A low growl came from the edge of the forest and a large wolf emerged into the moonlight, his teeth bared, bright white against the black of his fur. I could see the yellow eyes of others, flanking his heel, but they seemed hesitant to follow him.

Was this one challenging me? The wolf in me snickered and I knew she had my back if things escalated too out of control for only my human form to handle.

"Just say the word, Mena. He won't touch you. I swear it," Phoenix said.

I shook my head and took a confident step closer, not even bothering to palm any of the weapons he had loaded me with. "Stay where you are. You can't earn my respect for me."

"Just remember what I told you."

I never took my eyes away from the giant wolf. "I won't have to take him out. He's going to listen to me."

A fierce growl vibrated from the wolf's throat and his lips curled even farther up over his sharp-looking canines. It was obvious he didn't agree with me. My wolf, however, did.

I looked over his head to the woods behind him. I knew I was completely surrounded by the pack, and they would all hear me.

"My name is Mena and I am the new pack leader. I am not aware of the leadership my late husband enforced, but I can assure you… things are going to change."

The wolf nearest to me growled again and took a step closer. I ignored him, and that seemed to anger him even more. My guess was he was Marc's second in command and he aimed to knock me out from under the crown. That wasn't happening tonight.

"I've spoken with Phoenix, the Master Vampire, and we have decided to be allies. The war between his clan and my pack is over. I know it will be a slow process, but I believe we can reach out to other packs and clans and convince them that this is the right thing to do."

"It won't work!" a female voice said, and the blond chick that had decorated Marc's arm in the motel parking lot walked from the woods, immodest of her nudity. "We don't need you and your new way."

A short laugh escaped me. "Well, you're welcome to challenge me anytime if you think you can do a better job of leading this pack. Until then, you will do as I order you to do."

The girl was stunned speechless. I supposed she thought I would tuck my tail and run away from her confrontation. That wasn't going to happen. I still had a bone to pick with her, and I would have been elated if she had taken me up on the offer of a challenge, but she took a step back.

"No?" I said to her. "I didn't think so." Looking back to my audience, I continued. "I plan to be fair, but firm, and I will give you the utmost respect as long as I receive the same in return."

The black wolf crouched and then sprang toward me. I pulled the dagger from the sheath on my right thigh the same time his massive paws knocked me flat of my back on the road.

A short yelp filled my ears before his jaws could close around my throat in what was sure to be my imminent and gruesome end. I pulled my knees up and used my feet against his stomach to send him flying over my head.

Quickly jumping to my feet, I expected the beast to come at me again, but he wouldn't. Not tonight. Not ever again. The four-inch hilt was all that could be seen of the silver dagger in the center of the man's bare chest. There was no rise and fall, because he no longer breathed. There was no heartbeat, because he was dead. I had killed him.

Hot tears pricked my eyes and I fell to my knees beside the male and wept.

PHOENIX

Phoenix watched as at least seventy werewolves stalked toward Mena, and regretted not bringing more of his clan with him.

"No!" he shouted as he rushed toward her, but stopped in his tracks when each one of them began to shift back to their naked, human forms. They enclosed Mena and the fallen male in a tight circle and then they all dropped to one knee and began to chant, their heads dropping low in respect for their pack leader and the fallen warrior in her arms as she cried great tears of sorrow.

Phoenix wanted to comfort her himself, but he knew this to be a pack tradition. No matter the great plan of Mena's to make the vampires and werewolves allies, he knew he wouldn't be welcome. Not yet.

"You think she's going to be okay?" Jaxon's voice broke through Phoenix's concentration, and he found that he was smiling as he nodded.

"Yeah. I think she will be just fine."

"It's going to be quite the experience getting along with our enemies now. Do you think this was meant to happen all along?"

The pack began to stand and then they parted down the center. Mena was talking with a tall male, and then the guy bent and picked the body up from the pavement and cradled him to his chest, like a sleeping child.

Mena looked up and their eyes met. Even through her grief, she smiled at him.

"Yes," Phoenix said. "I do think this was meant to happen… all along."

ACKNOWLEDGEMENTS:

Editor: Ella Medler

Beta readers: *Dottie Schmeckpeper, Christy Mann, Jessica Parra, Amanda Wright, Third London, Katie Harder-Schauer*

Special Thanks to: Shawn and Riley for being my rock when I needed a little bit of reality to hold on to.

MEET THE AUTHOR

Kristie Haigwood (a.k.a. K.S. Haigwood) is currently writing her 10th novel. She lives in Arkansas, US. She is the mother of 2 awesome kids and 2 great dogs. She is happily married to her soulmate who thinks reading is a solid waste of time. Opposites attract. Kristie's works include 'Save My Soul', 'Hell's Gift', 'Good Side of Sin', 'Forbidden Touch', 'Eternal Island', 'Eternal Immortality' and 'Accepting the Moon'. 'Eternal Illusion', 'The Last Assignment', 'Midnight Moonrising' and 'My Sweet Purgatory' are all releasing soon.

VISIT ME ONLINE:

Facebook: www.facebook.com/kristie.haigwood
Twitter: http: @KSHaigwood
Blog: kshaigwood.blogspot.com
Fanclub: www.facebook.com/groups/kshaigwoodfanclub

Click on link below to join my mailing list!
www.facebook.com/kshaigwood/app_100265896690345

OTHER BOOKS BY KRISTIE

SAVE MY SOUL SERIES

SAVE MY SOUL — BOOK 1

Kendra Larkin had everything going in the right direction. Her life was seemingly perfect, and she wouldn't have changed a thing about it. Unfortunately, the course of her life was about to be forever altered. A tragic rappelling accident lands her on Dr. Adam Chamberlain's operating table.

She agrees to a deal proposed by a guardian angel to help save the soul of the man who is both her doctor and soulmate. If she is successful, she gets to keep her life. However, she later learns that it isn't just her life that's in jeopardy, but her soul as well.

Even with the help of her handsome guardian angel, Rhyan, it seems there is no happy ending in sight. Torn between her newly discovered love of Rhyan, and the undeniable attraction she has for Adam, Kendra finds herself at a crossroad. With Adam's steadfast rejection of God, and his guardian demon conspiring against her, she fears her soul may already be lost.

Will she find a way to overcome the evil her life is suddenly burdened with? Or will Adam's guardian demon win both their souls and make Kendra his own personal puppet in Hell?

HELL'S GIFT — BOOK 2

Depression consumes the guardian angel, Rhyan, after his human charge chooses her soulmate over him. Filled with anger and despair, he lashes out. And when his hate-filled words land him neck-deep in Hell, he realizes he's gone too far. He expects trouble, but not to discover his own soulmate in the fiery depths. Abigail is there with good reason, but she's done her time, and in order to save them both, Rhyan must strike a deal with the Devil. The stakes are higher than ever before, with his soul, his friends and even the fate of Heaven and Earth in jeopardy. If he fails, Rhyan stands to lose more than he ever feared. Will true love be denied? It will take everything he's got to break down the traps Lucifer puts in his way. New lines are drawn and old scores are settled, and Rhyan is in for the fight of his life. With Abigail as the prize, and humanity in the balance, he will stop at nothing to claim…Hell's Gift.

This novel contains explicit content of violence, descriptive sexual scenes and strong language not suitable for anyone under the age of 18

GOOD SIDE OF SIN — BOOK 3

Josselyn has just spent the last three months in intense Line of Defense training so she could join Malcolm's search party. Little did she know the archangels had no intention of letting her bring back into Heaven an angel who had opened a portal between Heaven and Hell, at least not before saving God's creations from the tight grasp of Lucifer first.

Three months have passed since the angel Rhyan released nine repented demons from Hell, and now innocent people are dying, but their souls are not going to Heaven. Josselyn's mission is to find the demon responsible for stealing the souls and bring it to justice before Lucifer gains enough power to rise and claim Heaven and earth as his own.

Her whole world is shaken when she discovers what tool Lucifer is using to track down the one key to the release of his eternal damnation. Thoros is one half-souled immortal she prayed she would never see again. The ex-Prince of Lust had stolen her heart and crushed it with a cheeky smile. Now, not only is she being forced to put her damaged ego aside and face the only man that has ever hurt her, but she has to work with him in order to complete her assignment.

Is she strong enough to keep from falling in love with him again? Or is their love the only thing that can keep Lucifer from getting the one thing he wants most? Heaven.

MY SWEET PURGATORY — BOOK 4
(COMING SOON)

ETERNAL ISLAND SERIES

ETERNAL ISLAND — BOOK 1

A place where vampires rule, witches play, danger lurks and dreams really do come true.

Eternal Island is a paranormal suspense novel, deeply rooted into myth. Vampires and magic form a unique backdrop to a love story with long reaching consequences. Human girl Ariana Lochalan finds herself transported from the relative calm of her Nowhere, Arkansas' life into a diametrically opposite existence when she discovers she is a powerful witch and meant to wed High Vampire of Eternal Island, Abe Cambridge. Despite first-sight magnetism, the two protagonists are being pushed apart, obstacles tripping them at every step, outside forces interfering and threatening their peace, and ultimately their lives. A world rich in magic and intrigue, Eternal Island is the first installment of a saga which has love at its core and delves through the mire that is human nature in a turmoil of feeling and emotion.

Would courage, resilience and love be enough to bring together two soul mates?

How much would you sacrifice to save the one who owns your heart?

ETERNAL IMMORTALITY — BOOK 2

Eternal Island is heaven on Earth. Love blossoms between witches and vampires, and none are happier than the King and Queen. Shortly after the wedding, the party is interrupted by a desolate plea. A man is in trouble, and soon an army is sent to his rescue — but is he who he claims to be?

Unbeknown to Abe and Ariana, a cauldron of trouble bubbles to the surface and terrible things begin to happen to innocent islanders. Dodging love triangles and intrigue, could the young Queen find the strength necessary to save her kingdom and the world, too? When the King begins to crumble and evil has won, would pure love be enough to save the whole of humanity from destruction?

Read this story with a Tiger's Eye stone in one hand and a strong faith in your heart. Cross your fingers and toes and hope for a miracle on Evil's finest winning day.

ETERNAL ILLUSION — BOOK 3 (COMING SOON)

STAND ALONES

FORBIDDEN TOUCH

Ciera has to break the ultimate vampire law to save Mitch, her mortal soulmate, from a terrible fate. Dane, the vampire who would do anything to win her affection, is responsible for Mitch being framed for murder. A fast chain of events is set in motion, which leads to the soulmates being torn apart and Ciera to lose her heart to the one person she has always despised, Dane. She finds herself completely in love with both men. But a rogue vampire puts them all in grave danger. Can she keep them both? Or will she have to accept one lover's sacrifice, to save the other?

MOONRISING SERIES

ACCEPTING THE MOON

MOONLIGHT RISING (COMING SOON)

DUE TO RELEASE DECEMBER 2014

MIDNIGHT MOONRISING

CHAPTER 1

MENA

Sharp January winds whipped my dark hair around my face, tangling the tresses and briefly blocking a reality I didn't care to face from my eyes. However, the cutting breeze wasn't what was chilling me to the bone. The icy gusts were actually quite warm compared to what I was being forced to deal with on this day.

Marc's funeral.

Over a hundred people crowded around the green canopy that covered the pastor, a dozen or so close friends and family members, including myself, and a coffin holding a dead werewolf pack leader.

Of course, Marc was no longer a werewolf. I had taken his life, as well as his position of pack leader, after he bit me and infected my body with lycanthropy. In other words, I was supposed to grow fur, two additional legs, a long snout, razor-sharp teeth, and howl at the moon every four weeks.

Keep the dog jokes to yourself. It hasn't happened—yet.

My predicament wasn't burying my husband, though; it was that I had to act like I actually gave a damn about the man that lay, still and lifeless, in the box in front of me. I had never been a very good actress, and lying had never come naturally to me, like it had Marc, so saying I was a bit nervous was an understatement. I just prayed the people who didn't know who my husband really had been would overlook my odd behavior as my own way of grieving. Nobody did it the same anyway.

Most of the warm bodies at the cemetery were my pack. The rest were lawyers and their spouses, people who worked at the firm and maybe a few—very few—family members.

I could tell a dozen or so of the seventy-eight pack members hated me and what I had done to their previous pack leader, but the majority seemed elated with the change in leadership. I hadn't had time to talk with any of them much; I had accepted the moon on Friday, and the funeral for

Chris, the werewolf who had challenged me and lost, had been on Sunday morning, and now Marc's ceremonial occasion was today, Monday

I was expected at the courthouse the following morning to give a statement to the press about how Marc was such a stand-up guy and always put others' needs before his own, blah, blah, blah, yadda, yadda, yadda—

I know what you're thinking. Why would they ask his wife to do something like that so soon after his death? That was actually my doing. Waiting a whole week wasn't going to happen. I needed it all behind me. Dead. Buried.

I stared at the beautifully crafted oak wood box in front of me, and thought, *Literally, I need you buried.*

I had changed so much in the past three days that I almost didn't know myself anymore. I knew it was *her*, my wolf, inside me, giving me strength mentally as well as physically. *She* had that whole 'no nonsense' attitude about life: if you can't do anything about it, then don't worry about it. *She* actually blocked that particular emotion from my brain, refusing to let me feel concern over things that were out of my hands.

Like Marc.

Like Chris.

I had murdered them both. Of course, both occurrences had been in self-defense on my part, but I doubted any judge would see things my way if I was ever accused. I couldn't tell the truth, and I didn't believe even my wolf was a good enough liar to keep us out of prison.

We couldn't go to jail. We *wouldn't* go. There was no possible way to hide my wolf from the system; my blood was tainted and different from any human's blood.

As it turned out, the coroner who had examined Marc and Chris, was one of my pack members, and had labeled Marc's death as homicide, and the pack had removed all his belongings from his body, so that it appeared he had been robbed before or after the murder occurred. The examiner wrote Chris's death off as a vehicle accident fatality. They put him behind the wheel of his own vehicle and shoved a shard of glass through his chest where the dagger had punctured his heart, and then rolled the vehicle off a cliff. I was sure glad the coroner wasn't one of the few who didn't like me.

"Don't look, but we got company—the bad kind," Daryn, a pack member, whispered by my ear.

Sneak Peek of 'Midnight Moonrising'

I struggled to keep my eyes focused on the pastor as he went on and on and on about how God had taken Marc from this earth, 'too early, much too young,' the pastor said. That was crap; I had taken Marc from this earth, and if you asked me, it was much too late.

I couldn't fathom who Daryn imagined to be the bad kind of company. I had thought vampires were the only enemy to werewolves, but I had formed an alliance with the Master Vampire of Montgomery, Alabama, and it was daylight to boot, so he couldn't be talking about Phoenix or any of his clan.

"Who is it?" I whisper-shouted over my shoulder, but Daryn didn't answer.

"Mrs. Hoke?"

Startled, I looked up to the pastor who was now standing in front of me. He smiled kindly and bent at the waist to take my hand. "I am deeply sorry for your loss, Mena. Marc is at peace now. Take comfort in the fact that he is with his creator. May the Father, the Son and the Holy Spirit fill you with comfort and peace that passes understanding. I am always here for you and your family in this time of despair, so please do not hesitate to contact me if you need anything. Go in peace, my child, and be comforted by the love of your God. I know Marc is smiling down and watching over you."

I just bet he's smiling, I thought, but what I said was, "Thank you, Brother Thomas." The idea that Marc was watching me gave me the heebie-jeebies, and a chill skittered up my spine. Could they not bury the body already?

I forced a small smile and he nodded, then walked away to greet one of Marc's uncles who had sat beside me during the services.

I took that as my cue to stand up and find Daryn, but when I turned, I was face to face with the city's homicide detective, Alex Rhodes.

Company—the bad kind. Crap!

Alex gave me a sympathetic expression as I slid my sunglasses into place over my eyes. "Mena, I'm so sorry to hear about Marc. All of us down at the precinct were blown away by the news. We're here for you. If you need anything at all, please don't hesitate to call me."

I sighed in relief, and my mouth curved up into a genuine smile. Alex and Marc hadn't exactly been friends. Marc had been a defense attorney, so the criminals the cops locked up, Marc had set them free. And he had been damn good at his job, too. I, however, had never had any problems with Alex; he had always been kind to me.

"Thank you, Alex." It was all I could think of to say, because the wolf inside me seemed to be mesmerized by the detective's hazel eyes, strong jaw line and that perfectly tousled brunette hair of his. I swear I thought she was drooling.

Embarrassed because I was staring at him, I tried to look away, but she wouldn't let me. I was happy I had remembered to put on my sunglasses; the hungry eyes of my wolf had to be showing.

No! I scolded her in my thoughts. *Not only is Alex off limits because he's a detective, but he's human! I'm supposed to be in mourning and you want to hump his leg! No. Sit down and let me get rid of him. He is dangerous to us.*

A shudder rippled through my body, and I could tell she wasn't at all happy with the way I had stood up to her, but I could feel her pouting and knew she was going to let me have my way—at least for now. I made a mental note to avoid Alex Rhodes at all costs.

"Can I give you a ride home? I—"

"Mena, the car is ready," Daryn's voice interrupted, and I could feel his anxiety as he moved into my personal space, the overgrown male crowding Alex in the process.

Alex observed him a moment and then casually took a step back, his hand coming up to offer an introduction. "Alex Rhodes. I don't believe I've seen you around Montgomery. Were you a friend of Marc's?"

Daryn eyed the outstretched hand and, instead of taking it, he brushed my lower back with his fingers and wrapped his arm around my waist, pulling me to him possessively.

I was in too much shock to respond. What the hell was he doing?

"Not really. Marc was my boss," Daryn said.

Those hazel eyes shifted from Daryn to me, and then Alex lowered his arm and nodded, seeming to understand something that was not true, that Daryn and me were dating, and going public with it at my late husband's funeral. No! That's the last thing I needed on the front page of the Daily Independent tomorrow, the same morning that I was to give the press release.

I lifted the heel of my left foot and casually placed it on the toe of Daryn's boot, then transferred the weight of my body onto it, aiming to cut one of his toes off if I was lucky.

Daryn's body went rigid and his arm dropped from around me.

Sneak Peek of 'Midnight Moonrising'

I smiled at Alex as Daryn limped away. "Sorry about that. He's my cousin and very protective of me. I guess he thought you were trying to make a move on me at my husband's funeral."

Oh, God! Where had that come from? I rolled my eyes as my wolf sniggered.

Alex took a cautious step back from me and gave me a sheepish grin as heat flooded up his neck. My wolf liked that. She liked that a lot.

Despite my wishes of staying away from Alex, my wolf forced my hand out to touch his arm. "Don't worry about it, Alex. I know you were only offering your condolences. Just ignore him."

He chuckled lightly as he scratched his eyebrow with his thumb. My wolf followed every move he made and encouraged me to notice that his ring finger on his left hand was free of any jewelry.

Of course, I already knew Alex was single, but him being unattached to anyone wouldn't help my wolf get her way, and I reminded her again that he was a detective—*the detective*—working Marc's murder case. She didn't understand that this guy would lock me up and throw away the key if he found out I was the one who killed Marc. It wouldn't matter if he had developed feelings for me.

"I, uh—call me if you need anything, Mena. I mean that… anything at all." His eyes narrowed and darted to the retreating Daryn, but he said no more on what transpired between the three of us.

My wolf resisted when I went to take my hand from Alex, but I caught her off guard and took a step back, well out of reach from the man. I gave him a small smile as I nodded, and then I turned and walked toward the line of vehicles.

Made in the USA
Middletown, DE
11 May 2021